For Jess xxx – C. H.

For Les – E. U.

BLOOMSBURY CHILDREN'S BOOKS
Bloomsbury Publishing Plc
50 Bedford Square, London, WC1B 3DP, UK
BLOOMSBURY, BLOOMSBURY CHILDREN'S BOOKS and the Diana logo are trademarks of Bloomsbury Publishing Plc
First published in Great Britain by Bloomsbury Publishing Plc

Text copyright © Caryl Hart 2018
Illustrations copyright © Edward Underwood 2018

A catalogue record for this book is available from the British Library

ISBN 978 1 4088 7304 5 (HB)
ISBN 978 1 4088 7305 2 (PB)
ISBN 978 1 4088 7303 8 (eBook)

1 3 5 7 9 10 8 6 4 2

Printed and bound in China by Leo Paper Products, Heshan, Guangdong
All papers used by Bloomsbury Publishing Plc are natural, recyclable products from wood grown in well managed forests.
The manufacturing processes conform to the environmental regulations of the country of origin.

To find out more about our authors and books visit www.bloomsbury.com and sign up for our newsletters

One Shoe
Two Shoes

Illustrated by

Edward Underwood

Written by

Caryl Hart

BLOOMSBURY
CHILDREN'S BOOKS
LONDON   OXFORD   NEW YORK   NEW DELHI   SYDNEY

One shoe

Two shoes

Red shoes

Blue shoes

Old shoes

New shoes

On their way to school shoes

Long laces tied in knots

Green pumps
with yellow spots

Party shoes

Arty shoes

Cowboy boots

Flip-flops!

Two shoes make a pair

Who's that hiding there?

Little mouse one
And little mouse two!

They've made a house
in someone's shoe!

A shoe
for a *house*?

A house
for a *mouse*?

A shoe
for a *house*?

Mouses houses
Red and blue

Slippers on the bedroom floor

Here's

little mouse

three

and little mouse four!

Five

six

seven

eight and nine

Ten little white mice

SHOES

All in line!

Scritchy scratchy

Who goes there?

Pitter
Patter

Sniff

Lick

SCATTER!

Doggy s t r e t c h

Good boy

Fetch!

Bounce away

Time to play

Hooray!